PUFFIN BOOKS
Editor: Kaye Webb
THE OWL HOOT
AT CATFISH BEND

This is the story of a happy community of
animals living on the banks of the Mississippi
in the paradise known as Catfish Bend—
happy, that is, until the day the gray fox, the
city slicker from New Orleans, with his
single shifty eye and voice like spilling
molasses, arrived and tearfully claimed the
Catfish Benders' hospitality. From that day
on, nothing was the same. Little by little the
five leaders of the community succumbed to
the wiles of the invader: Doc Raccoon, the
thoughtful mayor of Catfish Bend; Judge
Black, the kindly, motto-quoting blacksnake
who had become a vegetarian to live down
the snake's bad reputation; J.C., the shrewd
and sporty red fox from Memphis; the silly
rabbit, always chasing butterflies; and the
gloomy frog, always predicting the end of the
world. Then, in the name of progress, as
happens so often with less wise humans, the
gray fox became their dictator—and like
most dictators, soon involved them in a terrible
war.

Books by BEN LUCIEN BURMAN

THE OWL HOOTS TWICE AT CATFISH BEND

SEVEN STARS FOR CATFISH BEND

HIGH WATER AT CATFISH BEND

THE STREET OF THE LAUGHING CAMEL

THE FOUR LIVES OF MUNDY TOLLIVER

EVERYWHERE I ROAM

ROOSTER CROWS FOR DAY

BLOW FOR A LANDING

STEAMBOAT ROUND THE BEND

MISSISSIPPI

IT'S A BIG COUNTRY

CHILDREN OF NOAH

MIRACLE ON THE CONGO

BIG RIVER TO CROSS

BEN LUCIEN BURMAN, 1895 –

THE
OWL
HOOTS
TWICE AT
CATFISH BEND

Illustrations by ALICE CADDY

Puffin Books

Puffin Books: a Division of Penguin Books Ltd
Harmondsworth, Middlesex, England
Penguin Books Inc, 7110 Ambassador Road, Baltimore, Maryland 21207, U.S.A.
Penguin Books Australia Ltd, Ringwood, Victoria, Australia

First published in the United States by Taplinger Publishing Co., Inc., 1961
Published in Great Britain by Harrap 1967
Published in Puffin Books in Great Britain 1969
Reprinted 1974
Published in Puffin Books in the United States 1974

Copyright © Ben Lucien Burman, 1961

Printed in the United States of America

THE OWL HOOTS TWICE
AT CATFISH BEND

eeeeeeeeeeeeeeeeeeeeeeeeeeeeeeeeeeeeeeeeeeee

I WAS strolling through the swamp at Catfish Bend when I saw my old friend Doc Raccoon hurrying through the trees, with his usually ragged hair all slicked up like he was going to a wedding.

I called out to him, but he hardly turned his head. "I can't stop," he answered. "I've got to make a speech. I'm late and it isn't half ready."

A cottontail rabbit right behind pulled the young rabbit with him by the paw. "Walk faster," he said. "We want to get a good place."

The raccoon went down the river bank to a grassy meadow where some squirrels and groundhogs were already waiting. Pretty soon more animals hurried past me, foxes

and otters, and beavers and muskrats, with their fur all shiny like the raccoon.

And then the sky became full of birds, woodpeckers and bluejays, and owls and wild geese, all chattering and hooting and honking at the top of their lungs.

A blackbird swooped down and lit on my head, and started to pull out a beakful of hair.

"No time for that now," called a crow, and jerked the blackbird away.

The animals and birds joined the others

on the bank. And then the raccoon climbed on a stump and began to talk, though I couldn't hear what he was saying. And then he finished and the geese and owls honked and hooted again and the woodpeckers and the bluejays hammered on the trees, like they were all applauding. And then the birds and animals paraded in front of the raccoon, and after that I couldn't see anymore, they all crowded around so. But I heard what sounded like foxes, crying as if their hearts would break. And I knew it was time to go, because things were getting secret now, and it wasn't wise for a human to be around.

I came back a few hours later and most of the crowd was gone. And the raccoon was sitting by the river, taking a rest in the shade.

"I'm glad that's over," he said. "Making a speech always wears me out. . . . You wouldn't have any of those licorice drops you brought last time, would you? They're wonderful to give you strength fast."

I gave him a few from a bag and he chewed for a minute. "It's good candy," he said. "I like a candy that sticks to your teeth."

I waited for him to begin talking, because I know raccoons can't be hurried, but he didn't say anything. I put my hand in my coat to take out more of the drops, and some coins fell out of my pocket. One of them was a bright new dime, and I saw his brown eyes light, because raccoons love anything shiny.

"I'll trade you for that," he said. "I'm collecting those dimes. I've got four of 'em already."

He reached under the log where he had some things hidden—he had things hidden all over. And he pulled out some bits of broken glass and scraps of tin and a big brass key he'd found. "I've got some nice things here," he went on. "Maybe you could use one of these instead."

I gave him the dime and took the key so as not to hurt his feelings. "A key always comes in handy," I said. "You never know what you need to open."

I waited for him to talk again, but still he wouldn't begin, just sat there shining the dime on his fur.

I got tired at last, and looked off where the birds and animals had been parading. "What does it all mean?" I asked.

He took another licorice drop and chewed till it was only a wafer. "I don't know whether I ought to tell you. There's so much we're ashamed of. But I guess it's better if you have it right, instead of hearing all the rumors. It's The Anniversary."

I looked puzzled. "You mean the anniversary of something you want to remember?"

He swallowed the wafer and shook his head. "It isn't something we want to remember. It's something we want to forget," he said.

The raccoon began:

I

I KNEW from the beginning we should never have let him come to the Bend. You had only to take one look at him to know that it meant terrible trouble. I think if we could have told what was going to happen, with all the sorrow and suffering, we'd have all jumped into the river and drowned.

It was a day in June, one of those wonderful days when it's good to be alive. I was lying on my back near the big live oak tree where I stayed, looking up at the clouds passing by, and the giggly rabbit was doing the same. And Judge Black, the blacksnake, was sitting in the sun near me, giving advice to some young raccoons that I'd invited to the Bend for a visit. A little way off the beaver was bossing some animals cutting down trees to make a clearing and a bandstand so the frogs of the Indian Bayou Glee Club could have a better place to sing. They'd been getting so popular animals were coming from all over the Valley to hear 'em, and they needed more room. Our old frog was there with the Club and a new frog they called a blacksmith frog made a noise like a hammer hitting metal. And the other frogs were all trying to imitate him so they could do something the old frog had always wanted, sing the *Anvil Chorus* from *Il Trovatore*.

J.C., the red fox, who thought he knew a lot about music, turned his head to listen. "I don't like these fancy pieces," he said. "I wish the frog 'd stick to *Sweet Adeline*. Adeline's a song you can roll around in your throat."

And he started singing it very loud, hoping that they'd join him. But they didn't.

Along the bank some otters were trying to teach some young rabbits how to swim and taking 'em on their back for a ride on an otter slide they'd made, just like a chute-the-chutes. And the watchman goose was standing near, being a life guard in case anybody started drowning.

Judge Black took one of his slippery-elm cough drops and spoke to the young rac-

coons. "All is not gold that glitters," he said, with one of the mottoes he was always using. "A bad penny always comes back."

There was a swooping of wings overhead and the big eagle that was the king of the birds at the Bend flew down in front of me, and right after him there came an owl.

The eagle was old and bald as a stone. And he folded his big wings about him and talked in a voice solemn and slow. "I have to leave in a few days," he said. "They want me to pose for a new statue they're putting up in the Capitol at Washington. There are a couple of matters we ought to settle before I go."

The rabbit and the frogs had hurried off; they were scared of an eagle. But they needn't have been afraid. When you knew him he was really nice.

I've always gotten along fine with the birds myself. I stay up in the trees for hours, and a bird can help you a lot. And many a time I might have been caught if a bluejay or a crane hadn't flown over and told me a raccoon hunter was coming. Some of the animals didn't think like me, and there used to be plenty of quarrels. But since the birds had signed our pact not to fight, we all lived together like brothers.

I offered the eagle some wild cherries, and for politeness he took a bite. "It's this fruit

I've come to talk about," he said. "It's beginning to ripen in the swamp. There are the
cherries now and the strawberries, and later
there'll be the apples and peaches in the old
orchard that's gone wild. I've been thinking
we ought to work out some plan so there
won't be any argument. I thought it would
be fair if we let one tree belong to the animals, and let every other one belong to the
birds."

I didn't lose any time answering. "That's a fine idea," I said. "I'll go with you tomorrow and pick 'em out. We'll tie a feather to a tree if it's the birds', and scratch a clawmark on the bark if it belongs to us."

The eagle was pleased, and then he cleared his throat and looked a little embarrassed. "About the fruit trees on the farm at the edge of the swamp where the people are living. It isn't exactly our property, and maybe it wouldn't be legal to do the dividing. If a bird or an animal wishes to borrow an apple or a pear now and then, I think we should let his own conscience decide."

We talked a little longer about arranging get-togethers each month so the animals and birds could know each other better. And he told me if anything came up while he was away to see the owl, and then he got ready to leave.

Just then a woodpecker began hammering on a tree and the owl jerked back like he was shot. He was an old owl with a kind of pinched face and his beak and feathers shook a little all the time. I could see he was very nervous. "I wish you'd do something to these woodpeckers," he complained to the eagle. "I have to work at night. If I don't get my sleep in the daylight I'm done. You know my nerves have been bad ever since my family trouble. And this rat-tat-tat from morning to dark makes me jumpy as a grasshopper."

They flew away and I lay back in the sun, and everything was quiet again. The rabbit began playing some silly game he said he'd invented, pulling the petals off a daisy, and trying to tell if they'd be cooking carrots that night on the farm. Some flying squirrels began playing in the trees, seeing who could turn the most loop-the-loops between the branches. And some hoopsnakes came out and started a hoop race, rolling down a hill.

Judge Black went on talking to the young

raccoons. "Beauty is only skin deep," he said, with another of his mottoes.

All of a sudden there was a crashing in the brush, and a big gray fox came rushing out, and threw himself on the grass before us. "Save me!" he panted.

We have plenty of strange animals com-

ing to the Bend, but this time I was really surprised. He was almost twice the size of our red fox, J.C., but he looked really pitiful. He had only one eye, and the other was almost closed where something had hit him, so he could hardly see. His fur was covered with mud and briars, and everywhere there were raw cuts where he'd bumped against some barbed wire.

We washed him up and gave him ironwood to chew. And then we sent word to the snake doctor, the big dragonfly that takes care of sick animals. And the snake doctor came and stitched up the fox's wounds, and the fox hollered something awful. And then he began feeling better.

"I've run away from the Zoo in New Orleans," he said. "The keepers chased me up the river. But I threw 'em off the trail at Sugar Cane, the little town below the swamp. It's a miracle I'm alive. I know you don't know anything about me. But you can ask any of the animals in the Zoo. They'll tell you I'm quiet and never make trouble. I hope you'll let me stay at the Bend."

I didn't want to let him come. Now that he was cleaned up, you could see him better. And I didn't even like to be around him, he made you feel so creepy. His single eye was shifty and wicked as an alligator's; he'd never look at you straight. When he talked his voice was like molasses and his smile was like you were walking on oil. He made you

feel even his fancy whiskers and tail were
false.

I got to thinking about his missing eye,
and he must have read my mind.

"I lost it at New Orleans," he said. "In a
fight when I escaped before, and thirty two
dogs jumped me."

Judge Black I could see didn't like him
either. But since the Judge had been trying
to live down the snakes' bad reputation
sometimes he was really too soft-hearted.
"The motto of the Bend is we help each
other," he said. "I don't see how we can
keep him out."

But it was J.C., our red fox, who decided.
"I'll go his bond," said J.C. "He's lived in
a zoo so long he's really a city fox. Everybody knows a fox is the smartest animal
there is. And a fox must be a hundred times
smarter when he knows city ways. There
are all kinds of things he can teach us."

Well, we'd let the watchman goose and

the beaver stay when they were in trouble. So we said we'd let him stay, too.

There was another noise in the bushes now, and a rat came running out, one of those wharf rats almost big as a dog that you see around the towboat docks on the river. You could tell this rat was a terrible gangster, with one whole side of his face knocked in from the fights he'd had and two of his front toes twisted sideways. He was all scratched and muddy like the fox, and he looked and talked so sad even the rabbit that always ran from a rat was almost crying.

"I came up with the fox from New Orleans," he said. "They've started a big rat exterminator campaign on the docks and I've lost my wife and all my family. I'm all alone in the world with no home and no friends. I've got nothing to live for. I went out to the Zoo and I met the fox and he asked me to run off with him. I don't ever want to see New Orleans again. Since the exterminators came New Orleans isn't New Orleans any more."

He chewed a green apple core I gave him, and then went on talking. "I'm no good to anybody since. It seems to have affected my mind. But if you let me come in, I can do day labor, clean up the paths and pick up the garbage, and any unpleasant thing you want done. If you say no, there's nothing left. I'll have to go back to New Orleans and let the exterminators gas me."

Well, some rats are nice, field rats and white rats and some of the swamp rats too. But those wharf rats are tough, and this one I could see was especially bad. But some of the animals said a city rat, like a city fox, could teach us a lot of things we needed to know, like how to stay out of the way of automobiles or maybe how to open the door of the ice-box they'd bought on the farm.

So after talking it over we told him our answer was yes.

Next morning when we gathered for breakfast the rabbit was white as milkweed. "We've made a dreadful mistake," he said, and he didn't have his usual silly giggle. "I had a horrible dream last night. A lot of gray foxes and rats had me all tied with vines. And they had a machine like I've seen when a carnival comes to Sugar Cane, with a hole in the top where they drop a ball and a lot of mouths with numbers at the bottom where the ball rolls out, and the person that gets the lucky number wins a prize. Only in this machine they'd drop me instead, and at each mouth a fox or a rat 'd be waiting. They dropped me a hundred times I guess, and then the gray fox said he'd won me. And then he grabbed me and I woke up. And there sure enough the fox was standing by me with the rat, and I think he'd been nibbling at my toe."

Judge Black ate some of his cereal, and let it slide down his long throat. "It's unfair to brand an animal a criminal so fast," he said. "I think you ate too much carrot salad."

I went out that day with the eagle like I'd said, and we marked the trees, and then I told him goodbye.

And I came back and saw the fox and the rat sitting around. And I knew that for once Judge Black was wrong.

For a little while they were both getting well, and everything went along all right. The fox 'd come in his slippery way and tell me how wonderful it was in the swamp. Or he'd slink up to Judge Black and say, because he knew snakes liked eggs and the Judge was important. "There's some fine bluejay eggs in a nest low down in that locust tree. Can't I go over and steal you a couple?"

Of course he didn't know that the animals and the birds had signed the Pact or that the Judge was a vegetarian. And everywhere

the rat 'd follow right behind, talking the same oily way.

And then in a couple of weeks they both began to change. They started to act superior. The fox 'd go around criticizing all the time and making fun of everything in the Bend. "Now when I was down at the Zoo in New Orleans we used to do it like this," he'd say. "The way you animals behave here at the Bend is just common hillbilly." And whatever the fox said, the rat repeated like an echo. And he'd chew a few grains of corn and roll 'em in his mouth, and spit 'em out, just like I've seen men chew tobacco.

And I guess our animals didn't have much sense, even some of the raccoons. They'd look at the two of 'em and say, "They're from the city and terribly smart. If they say so, it must be right."

Well, the fox told us to clean up around the trees like it was at the Zoo, so they'd grow better and make the swamp like a park. And that was good and made things easy when the nuts fell; you didn't have to search so hard in the grass.

And then he came on a mole digging through the earth, and of course it couldn't see. "It's bad having an animal like that," he said. "We'd never have allowed it in the Zoo. From now on we'll give each mole a mouse to show him the way, like the dogs they have for blind men in town."

And the poor blind moles were very happy. And everybody said how lucky we were the fox and the rat had come to stay.

And then there were a couple of things that got me awfully worried. The gray fox didn't like birds, whether they lived in the trees like the bluejays or the crows, or in the reeds like the cranes and the herons. "They're only good for eggs," he'd say. "Their voices hurt my ears, and their feathers make me sneeze."

The watchman goose came up one day when I was walking with Judge Black. "I don't like it," he said. "The gray fox sits and stares at me and his eye gets all glassy. He's getting ready to hypnotize me and have me for dinner. A fox can hypnotize a goose, just like a snake does a frog. That was one of the first things I learned when I was training to be a watchman."

Judge Black looked hurt. "Would you mind not talking about snakes and hypnotizing?" he asked. "I've tried to forget those things long ago. Ever since I became a vegetarian."

I looked at the gray fox next time he passed the goose. And I didn't have to look any more. And after that I slept next the goose every night.

The fox liked fruit, and when he saw a wild cherry tree marked with a feather he'd pay no attention, except when I was around. But he was really crazy about bird eggs, and the rat was just as bad. A couple of times I caught them robbing a nest, and I reminded them of the Pact, and stopped them in a hurry.

I was out in the woods one day when I heard a big commotion. And I ran over and saw the fox and the rat in an awful fight. They'd started to rob a bluejay's nest, and the bluejays and some crows and other birds that were around were trying to drive them away.

There's one crow that I know pretty well.
I saved him once when he was a young bird
and an alligator almost got him. He talks too
much, and he'll steal from me if he gets a
chance because crows like shiny things
worse than a raccoon. And he's got other
bad habits, too. But he's all right and he's
done me plenty of favors, showing me black-
berries I couldn't see myself and telling me
where he'd seen hunters setting traps.

Well, this crow was with the birds fighting the fox and the rat, when I saw the fox
make a quick jump and catch him. And he'd
have been gone if I hadn't rushed up and
called out to the fox to stop.

The fox dropped the crow fast and stood
looking foolish. And I waited till the birds
flew off, and then I told him and the rat
what I thought.

"That's the last of egg stealing," I said.
"These birds are our friends. Remember
you're only invited here. If this happens

anymore I'll see that you leave at once."

The fox brushed a crow feather from his mouth. "I'm sorry," he said. "I didn't know. I'll never touch an egg again."

I started to leave and he put on his alligator smile. But when I turned around he and the rat were showing their teeth.

II

*T*HAT NIGHT I couldn't sleep, thinking, and I heard an owl hoot twice. It's always scary to hear an owl hoot that way because it always means trouble is coming. The owl kept it up, long mournful hoots, that made your blood freeze over. And then suddenly it gave an awful cry, and didn't hoot any more.

I was sure something was wrong and next day I went to ask the crow.

I found him where a lot of crows were sitting on the ground, as gloomy as their black feathers. They weren't even eating the rice they'd brought in from a field for their lunch.

He took me off to the tree where he lived and began searching in his nest, full of

strings and bottle caps and scraps of colored rags. Crows' nests are always a jumble. "My sister's lost a couple of eggs," he said. "I let her and her husband stay in this nest some summers and she thinks she may have laid 'em here. She's dreadfully absent-minded. I've looked but I can't find anything in all this awful tangle."

I asked him what caused the owl hooting. He looked gloomier than ever. "That's why we're all in low spirits," he said. "We crows are good ourselves at telling bad weather and trouble. But there's an old lady owl lives over there in the tree is the best prophet around. She's never wrong about knowing when bad things are coming. She told about the hunters taking the Bend and the big tornado at Vicksburg. Last night she was talking about the things she saw ahead. And then she saw something coming to the swamp so terrible she fainted right in the middle. We asked her this morning what it was, but she won't tell anybody."

The animals at the Bend heard about it, too, and worried for a while, and then put it out of their minds. And then they started talking about the fox again and all the fine things he was going to do.

Each time the fox heard the animals say anything he'd get more and more conceited. He began thinking he was handsome now, and plenty of times you could see him sitting by a pool, looking at himself in the water. And he'd slick back his hair and fluff out his tail till it looked like some queer kind of gray flower. "I'm proud of this tail," he'd say if you happened along. "It comes from my old family in Virginia. I guess you've heard of the fox hunts of Virginia. My father and grandfather and his father before him were the foxes that raced in the hunts."

Well, he had two or three more good ideas. And one day he stopped where a rabbit was digging a hole, and watched the earth flying outside. "These dirt holes are so old-fashioned," he said. "The dirt's always falling and they're so hard to clean. When I was down at the New Orleans Zoo all our holes were what they call concrete, white and smooth as eggshell. I see the government men are building a new flood wall down by Turtle Crossing. Why don't you steal some of the concrete after they've quit work and put it around your hole?"

Well, the rabbit went down after the men were gone, and made a lot of trips back and forth and plastered the concrete inside. And the rest of the rabbits and most of the other animals that lived in holes did the same. For a while they all thought it was fine, it was so easy to brush out every day. And you could almost see the fox's head getting bigger. And then one day the first rabbit started sneezing and coughing. And pretty soon all the animals had dreadful colds and every hole that you passed was like a towboat popping off steam. The snake doctor came and he said some of 'em had pneumonia, and he sent for more doctors to help. And they had to work night and day to keep the animals from dying.

I was sure that would finish him, but it wasn't the way I thought. A few of the animals tried to take the concrete out, and of course they couldn't, so they dug themselves a new hole. But most of 'em kept coughing and wouldn't change for anything. The fox had said concrete was the style.

I couldn't help making fun of them for being so foolish, and all of our crowd did, too. And J.C., who was fine at acting, did an imitation of the gray fox. He'd strut back and forth, swishing his tail, and say, "Now when I was down at the New Orleans Zoo," and then he'd suddenly start coughing and cough till he almost burst. And we'd laugh till we choked.

You can imagine I did plenty of talking wherever I went. And then one day J.C.

hurried up to me, and this time I could see he wasn't being funny.

"I just heard," J.C. said. "The gray fox is plotting against you. He's planning to push you out and take over the Bend. He won't stop at anything, even violence. I know. I'm a fox myself. He's a dangerous animal."

"Just let him try," I said. "He'll end up differently than he thinks."

Judge Black nodded he agreed. "Give a rogue rope enough and he'll hang himself," he said.

I kept my ears open after that but I didn't hear any more.

You'd have thought the gray fox would slow down a little after what happened with the concrete. But he went on strutting around just the same, telling about his family from Virginia, and how he lost his eye when the thirty two dogs jumped him. And one day I saw him looking at a tree where a

squirrel was sitting in his hole. "You animals are foolish with just one hole to a tree,"
he said. "When I was down at the Zoo we
had all the holes together, like people in the
cities. Think of the time and the steps it
saves if you want to visit a friend or you're
sick and need a neighbor."

Well, you might not believe it but they all
did what he said again. Everywhere you
could see animals digging and boring. I tried
to stop 'em, but nobody 'd listen.

"I can't figure it out," I said to Judge
Black. "I don't want to use the word if it
bothers you. But it's like they're hypnotized."

It used to be so peaceful and quiet in the
swamp. But now instead of one hole in a
tree there'd be thirty or forty. It was really
awful. Hundreds of children running all
over and knocking your eyes out if you
weren't careful, throwing nuts and stones.
And at night when you were asleep animals

'd walk over you at any hour, getting up to go to work. And once in a while an animal 'd get mixed up with all the holes looking exactly alike, and he'd say to himself, "It's the fourth from the top." But it'd be the fifth instead. And he'd climb in and fall on top of you, just when you were dreaming of trees full of persimmons.

And then one morning the crow came flying over, all excited. "I've got some news," he said. "I met a heron yesterday that had just been down in New Orleans, and he'd been talking to some birds in the Zoo. They told him the gray fox didn't come from Virginia at all, and he hadn't lost his eye in battle. He was a hillbilly from Arkansas, and he'd lost his eye when he hit it on a wire stealing a couple of chickens."

We laughed and laughed and J.C. did his imitation again.

"I'll write a poem about it," giggled the rabbit:

"The gray fox said he was a hero.
But really he was zero."

He had a lot more verses, he said, but we shut him up in a hurry. The rabbit sometimes was just too silly.

Of course crows are the worst kind of gossips. Soon everybody in the Bend knew the story. But it didn't seem to make any difference.

I quarreled with the gray fox every time we met. I was out in the woods one day and I saw him and the rat start eating some apples on a tree that was plainly marked with a feather.

"Keep off," I said. "You know that belongs to the birds. I marked it myself with the eagle."

And he and the rat slunk away.

J.C. came to me next day, and he was looking pale. "I told you that fox was dangerous," he said. "He's going wild. He says you block him in everything, that you won't even let him eat a sour apple. He doesn't want to face you in the open. But he's talking about sending to New Orleans for some gangster rats like the one that's here to do away with you."

Well, it looked like it was nothing but talk, and the rats didn't come. But the rat that was at the Bend began showing his real gangster character. Instead of chewing corn, now all the time he'd act tough and chew matches. If some animal didn't do just what the gray fox wanted, he'd roll the matches in his teeth. "I'll burn you out," he'd growl. And knowing how rats love to gnaw matches and set a house on fire, they could tell he wasn't just talking.

Only when I or Judge Black was around he'd change his tune, because he was still afraid of me, and rats are scared to death of blacksnakes.

"I was only fooling," he'd say.

And Judge Black 'd just stare with that

icy look of his when you'd done something wrong, and he'd say, "If a fool's hat fits you, wear it."

And the rat 'd stand there shivering and chewing. And once he got so nervous he set his own mouth on fire.

And then the fox started the bank. Before he came each animal had his own hole where he kept things, nuts and seeds and shiny stones and the coins people dropped at a picnic. But the fox said it was unsanitary having things like that right in the same place where you lived and slept, besides taking up so much room. And he said they'd start an animal bank, one big hole where everybody kept his belongings. They made the bank of a big tree that was hollow almost to the bottom, and everybody brought what they owned and put it all inside. And the fox put the rat on guard to keep order.

Well, it was easy enough bringing things. But getting 'em out was different. Everything got mixed up. One squirrel 'd put away some fine walnuts and he'd get some that were all wormy. And one raccoon 'd put in a half dollar that somebody 'd lost in the woods and he'd shine it up like a mirror. And when he'd go to get it out, he'd find somebody else had taken it first, and left an old rusty penny. And then there'd be a big quarrel. You could always tell when you were coming near the bank by all the yelling and fighting.

I tried to argue with the other animals, but the way I said, it was like a terrible sickness had 'em.

"I had another nightmare," said the rabbit one morning when we all sat down to eat. "I dreamed I was in a lovely place with beautiful flowers growing in the fields and butterflies floating everywhere. And all of a sudden it turned dark and began to rain. You've heard people say it rained cats and dogs. Only this time it rained rats and foxes. One rain drop 'd be a big wharf rat and the other 'd be a gray fox. And then everything—"

"Please spare us any more of your dreams," said J.C. "You're spoiling my breakfast."

And then something happened that made me realize I'd have to act fast.

A truck going down from Memphis had

dropped a whole big sack of paper-shell pecans. And we got 'em and we'd never tasted any nuts so wonderful; they were so sweet and so easy to crack. Everybody ate a few of 'em, and then brought the rest to the bank, to keep for special days and for the old animals who didn't have teeth and couldn't crack regular nuts except with a stone. And then the pecans began to disappear from the bank, and pretty soon they

were all gone. And then other things couldn't be found. And everybody was looking for the animal that was taking 'em, and saying what they'd do when he was caught.

One morning I was passing a tree off from the rest where I had a big hole I hadn't been to for a while, and I saw fox and rat paw marks all around it. And I looked inside and there were the paper-shell pecans and all the coins and the pieces of glass that were missing. It was filled to bursting. The fox and the rat had taken the things from the bank and put 'em in my hole. And then they were going to bring the animals and show 'em I was the thief.

As soon as it was dark I got the Judge and we carried everything back to the bank.

And then in the morning I called all our crowd for a council. "This can't go on any longer," I said. "Nobody will be safe."

"You can't tell what he'll do next,"

croaked the frog. "He's started to break up the Glee Club. He told me it was wrong for a frog to sing just one note. He said I ought to teach 'em to sing a whole scale, like a cat."

"I heard him," said the rabbit. "And his language was shocking."

The folds in the old frog's face hung down gloomy as clouds before a storm. "I didn't do what the fox asked," went on the frog. "And now every day he takes the stuffed skin of a cottonmouth snake and pokes it out of the bushes where we practice, and we jump for our lives. Or he puts a muskmelon near us, and we think it's a cottonmouth again, because muskmelon's the way a cottonmouth smells. The whole Club is going to ruin. They can't keep time anymore."

The rabbit shivered. "There was a real cottonmouth yesterday. He'd have swallowed me if the watchman goose hadn't been around. And then the goose made him talk and he said it was the gray fox that told him to come."

"An animal is known by the company he keeps," Judge Black declared.

They talked back and forth till the sun was high above the trees and everybody grew quiet.

I sat watching some yellow butterflies floating over a lily pool and then I spoke at last. "The animals 'll have to make a choice," I said. "It's either the gray fox or me."

After that we went around the swamp, talking to every animal we knew. But I wasn't really worried. I didn't think there'd

47

be much doubt about who they'd pick after all I'd done for the Bend.

The day came when we were to choose, and all the animals, the otters and the squirrels, and the foxes and the rabbits, and the woodchucks and the muskrats, gathered in front of the live oak tree where I had my home.

"Let's have the vote," I said. "Everybody that's for me stand under the oak. If they're on the fox's side let 'em stand over there under the burned pine tree."

They began shuffling around and a few of 'em hesitated, going under one tree and then another. But when they finally stopped there were only seven by the oak, just my old faithful friends, the watchman goose and the frog and the rabbit and the beaver, our own red fox, Judge Black and me.

III

FROM THAT time on the gray fox was the boss of everything.

One night not long after we were walking in the woods when I heard a funny sound. I stopped and heard it again, a queer crackling in the brush.

"We're being followed," I said.

The watchman goose twisted his neck in a figure 8 and stuck out his head to listen. "You're right," he said. "They're just be-hind the trees. It must be the gangster rats that he's hired to kill us."

I'd heard rumors that three rats had come up from New Orleans that day. And we drew back in the shadows and waited. Pretty soon they came along, three awful sewer rats with shoulders big as bulls and eyes like

red hot needles. And they passed so close I could feel their breath on my fur.

"We'll get the raccoon first," said the biggest rat. "I know a place down in Baton Rouge where we can sell his skin for plenty."

The second one gave a grunt. "Raccoon's worth nothing these days. The red fox is the one that's money."

The third one didn't say anything. He just looked horrible.

They went on through the woods.

The old frog was in a panic. "Darkness

and doom," he croaked. "We'll never get home alive."

We got back to the camp all right. But the next day it was the same, wherever we went there was always something behind.

"We'd better move off to ourselves," I said. "Where we can be ready for anything."

There was a kind of little corral made of logs the farm people that used to live in the Bend had built there years ago. There wasn't much room but the walls were high. And it was near my old tree where you could see anybody coming. So we cleaned it out and got the beaver to chop a few trees to put where the logs had rotted away and fixed it up like a stockade. And we stayed in it every night with somebody always on guard.

Now that I'd left, the gray fox took over the live-oak, and I'd see him sitting where I always sat and it made me very sad.

A few days passed and the three rats

didn't seem to do anything to hurt us. I couldn't figure it out. And after a while we got so used to 'em following us we hardly knew they were there.

And then the gray fox started with the eggs again. Wherever I'd go for a walk I'd see the rat climbing a tree and throwing down eggs for him to catch. And of course the other animals started doing it, too. And everywhere possums and squirrels were tossing eggs like they were playing ball. And they'd come down from the branches licking their chops, with their noses and ears all yellow. And then the bird 'd fight back, and a lot of birds and animals got hurt. They'd quarrel over the fruit, too, when the animals took the trees marked with a feather. There was hardly a day when you didn't see the snake doctors going around after some kind of battle.

The crow talked to me about it a couple of times, but I told him I was helpless. And then I didn't see him any more, and I heard he had gone away.

One day I was out with Judge Black and I saw the rat climb to a nest way up at the top of a tall pine tree.

"Watch close," I said to the Judge. "If he touches that nest he'll be sorry."

The rat scrambled in and threw down an egg so big it looked like a melon. The gray fox caught it all right, and started to crack it with a stone, when the rat came down the tree so fast he whistled like a bullet. And a minute later a lady eagle was flying around, flapping her wings, and screeching. And the rat started running across the field and the fox came racing after. They had robbed the nest of the big eagle that was the king of the birds in the Bend. The rat jumped into a hollow log on the ground and the fox was right behind him. But the hole was too small for a big animal like the fox and all his back and his tail were showing.

"My husband generally takes care of animals like you!" the lady eagle screamed. "But he's away, posing for the statue in Washington. I'll teach you to rob the nest of an eagle!"

She began nipping at the fox's tail with her beak, and pulling out chunks of fur. And then he couldn't stand it anymore, and popped out backwards from the log, and went hollering toward the river. And all the bluejays and the blackbirds and the woodpeckers that were up in the trees nearly burst off their feathers laughing.

The fox got back to his camp at the live oak and started pacing back and forth like a panther. He paced that way until it got dark, and then he paced all night. And when the sun rose he called all the animals together. "We've been putting up with these insults long enough," he said. "We'll start a war and drive every bird from the Bend. We'll begin training an army tomorrow."

He started next day like he said, and under every tree and in every grassy place you could see animals marching and drilling. He showed 'em how to get up on a branch and pull a bird's tail feathers; he showed 'em how to dodge down a hole when a hawk came

diving. He made the wharf rat that was his
friend a general, and then he got some mink
for assistant generals because their tempers
were bad and they had such pretty coats.
And then he brought more rats from New
Orleans, and he picked the ones that had

nice whiskers and made them generals and colonels. There were all kinds of animals for regular soldiers, squirrels and ferrets and weasels and skunks, but mostly they were possums. Our old frog said the possums were so dumb and always half asleep and asked me why the fox had so many for soldiers. And I said I guessed it was so the officers would seem bright.

All day the fox kept giving the animals commands. "Claws in. Claws out. Scratch." "Teeth right. Teeth left. Bite." And the woods around were so scarred with the marks some of the young trees died.

We'd watch and think how different it used to be when we had the Pact.

"This would be about the time when we'd be having the big picnic," sighed the rabbit. "With the rabbit-jump contest and the chipmunk races to see who could run fastest with the most nuts in his mouth."

J.C. brightened. "And the race where

we'd borrow the garbage can from the farm and see who could get the lid off the quickest. That was a wonderful day."

But there weren't any contests or races now.

The gray fox made the animals go out and steal fruit and eggs even if they weren't hungry. Or they'd break the eggs in the nests, just to make the birds wild. The birds fought back harder now, and sometimes they'd carry off a baby skunk or a squirrel. And then the fox would say that when he was finished nobody 'd know what a bird looked like in over a hundred miles.

There were always a lot of bats flying around. And one twilight I saw a little bat that I knew hanging upside down on a branch like bats do, and even upside down I could see he was crying. When I asked the reason he started crying harder. "I'm a bat," he sobbed. "With all this fighting I can't tell which side I'm on, whether I'm a bird or an animal. My wings flutter and I start to stay with the birds. And then I give a squeak, and that's the mouse in me coming out, and I fly away to help the animals."

Well, things kept getting worse and worse. And then I heard the eagle was back and had sent word to the gray fox he was coming next morning to talk things over. And the news made me happy again. Eagles are terrible fighters, and I knew he'd put the fox in his place.

Next morning came fast, and I could see the fox was really scared. He was sitting in front of the live oak with the rats and the mink and some possums around him, not saying a word, just waiting. Pretty soon birds started coming overhead, so thick their wings blackened the sky. And then the eagle flew down and after him the old owl. And the fox watched and the rat chewed matches, and got ready for a fearful battle.

The eagle and the owl walked up to the

fox, and the eagle looked more solemn than ever. "I've just returned from Washington," he said. "I should have been back sooner. But when I got through posing for the statue they asked me to stay a little longer. They want to put me on a new twenty five cent piece they're making."

He looked embarrassed for a moment—I knew he got embarrassed easily. "I hear that when I was away my wife created a little disturbance. I'm afraid she has a bit of a temper. Myself I'm getting old and I'm bald before my time. I've had enough fighting in my life. I don't want any more trouble."

The old owl's beak and feathers were shaking now like he had chills and fever, and one eye kept opening and shutting like somebody was pulling it with a string. "I can't stand this fighting either," he complained. "The woodpeckers were bad enough. But with this quarreling and stealing all the time I never get a chance to sleep a minute. I shake like I've got St. Vitus dance. And just yesterday I got this twitch in my eye. My nerves are going to pieces."

The eagle fanned himself with a wing. "It's unusually hot," he said. "Looks like tornado weather. . . . I've been talking things over with the other birds. And we've decided. We try to be fair and we like peace and quiet. If you promise to stop bothering our eggs we'll give you this whole half of the swamp, everything on this side of the sandy ridge that cuts the swamp in two. That way you can have all the fruit and anything else to yourselves. As soon as we can get the things in our nests packed up, we'll move out to the other half, and won't even fly over here any more."

Well, you could have heard a spider jump. For a minute nobody spoke a word. The fox and the rat just sat and stared at that terrible beak and claws they knew could have torn them to pieces.

And then our frog gave a dismal croak. "Doom," he moaned. "Doom and disaster."

And then the fox smiled his slippery smile, and said of course he'd do what the eagle wanted. And the rats and the mink and the other animals gave a cheer, and the eagle and the birds flew away.

Well, in a couple of days the birds were all moved out. And after that you couldn't hold the fox. He'd walk around the camp and every minute he'd look up at the sky where there wasn't a single bird flying. And the rats and the mink would tell him how wonderful he was, and he'd fluff out his bushy tail.

He kept the animals drilling, though; I couldn't figure out why. And the three sewer rats were still always behind us, following us like our shadows.

We were sitting in front of our stockade one twilight—We didn't often close the gate because the place was so small and so hot—

And the little bat I knew came and hung himself upside down in a tree, and I could see his eyes were red again from crying. "I still can't make up my mind," he said. "If it keeps on like this both sides 'll hang me as a spy."

"Would you mind sitting up straight?" I

asked. "When you're upside down it's a little difficult talking."

He swung upward in a hurry. "I'll have to talk to you fast," he said. "I can't stand straight up this way except for a minute. It makes all my blood run the wrong way, and 'll make me forget what I came for . . . Bird or animal a friend's a friend. I came over to warn you. I was just flying around where the fox was talking to the rat. He's planning some new kind of trouble with the birds and wants you and your crowd out of the way. He's been hoping the three sewer rats 'd scare all of you and make you leave the Bend. But now he's not hoping any longer. He's planning to capture you one by one and take you down to the Big Marshes along the Gulf and let the ocean waves drown you."

Well, we went inside the stockade and pulled the gate shut, and kept it closed all night. But the weather was scorching and it was terribly cramped. So when nobody came to attack us next day we left the gate open again. But I kept sharp watch just the same.

The old frog was in an awful state. "We're finished," he moaned. "There's no use doing anything. I should have stayed with the Club at Frogmore where I was born and never listened when they asked me to lead the Club at the Bend."

And then the terrible things began to happen. The watchman goose was the first. He'd been wonderful, that goose. He never once fell asleep the way he always did before he came to the Bend, when the geese threw him out for sleeping on duty. At night he'd march up and down in front of the gate, humming to himself to keep awake. And sometimes he'd ask the bat to go off to the farm and bring him some of the coffee grounds they'd thrown outside, and he'd chew 'em all the time because he'd heard

people say coffee 'd keep you awake. The
gray fox tried to get him away from the gate
by insulting him, and reminding him how
the geese had kicked him out for napping.
And then the fox put animals in front of the
gate, all pretending to be asleep, and snoring.
And one night he brought half a dozen possums instead, and they didn't need any pretending. They were all asleep in a minute.
And the goose gave a yawn, and then he
was scared, and he started chewing coffee
grounds fast.

The gray fox kept the possums there, and the goose began to look desperate. He spoke about his troubles next time the bat came over. "It's hard on me seeing those possums stretched out with their eyes closed, so happy. Will you fly over to the farm and bring me some more coffee grounds? I'm running out."

He managed for a few times after that, and I guess he'd have been all right. But the farm people went off to Memphis to stay awhile, and the coffee grounds were finished. I woke up a couple of nights later with that queer feeling that something was wrong. And I rushed to the gate and I didn't have to look twice—the watchman goose was gone. We went outside and searched and searched. But we couldn't find a trace. And then it was the beaver. There were always rats and mink and possums surrounding us now, and sometimes the gray fox would come himself. And then we decided we'd have to make the stockade bigger so we could have more room to move around. Of course the beaver was the one that cut down the trees. He always cut them so they fell straight now, not like the time before he came to the Bend, when the other beavers threw him out because he always made the trees fall crooked. He always carried a little stone to sharpen his teeth and he'd traded a new one a while before from a beaver that came swimming down the river.

"This is the best stone I've ever had," he

said. "I can keep my teeth sharp as a razor. I wish those beavers that threw me out could see me now. I think they'd apologize."

He was chopping and sawing, making the stockade so strong we could fight off a hundred times our number. He was so proud of himself it made you smile. And he came to a big pine, and was sawing hard when all of a sudden he gave a shout.

"Look out! It's falling wrong!" he cried, and gave a jump backwards. But he couldn't jump fast enough, and the top branches caught him like a trap. And before we could rush up the rats and mink had carried him away. In a few seconds we were after 'em, but they had too good a start and there were too many holes where to hide. We gave up at last, and I looked at the tree, and I saw why it had fallen wrong. It wasn't the fault of the beaver. His cutting had been fine. But the rats and the other animals had sawed the other side of the trunk and then covered it up so you couldn't see the marks; the tree was almost cut through.

Without the beaver we had to stop building the new stockade. And so many rats and mink were around us now it was like we were in a jail. Our food was running low, too. There wasn't anything left but a few nuts and some sunflower seeds we'd brought. I told Judge Black to divide 'em because I knew he'd divide 'em fair.

He made them into five little piles. "We'll manage somehow," he said. "Half a loaf is better than no bread."

We sat down to eat and I cracked a nut, and I saw it was all wormy. And then every nut turned out the same way. So there were only the seeds. One day I saw my reflection in a pool of rain-water. And I wouldn't have known myself. I was nothing but skin and bones.

And then the gray fox started having his meals right outside the stockade to torment us. He'd sit down with the rats and some of the mink, and eat sweet potatoes and honey and corn. And sometimes he'd bring milk or a pie he'd stolen from the farm. And they'd eat and laugh and sometimes throw us a scrap because they knew a taste would make us feel worse.

I noticed that J.C. was acting queer, and I began to get worried. He'd look through a crack at the gray fox eating, and then he'd sit moping in a corner. I tried to say something funny to make him laugh, but he wouldn't answer a word. And all night he'd stalk up and down with his face all stony, like he was walking in his sleep.

One night he was on guard and I waked with a noise and saw him peeping through the logs. And I looked, too, and saw the gray fox on the other side, and I just lay quiet and listened.

"You don't belong with this crowd, J.C.," the gray fox was saying. "You're too important an animal. With you and me working together we can take over the whole Mississippi Valley. Come and join me and you won't be sorry. I've got a fat goose waiting for you right now."

I could see J.C.'s mouth watering. And then a sad look came over his face, and he shook his head, and began guarding again.

Next day the gray fox was outside with the rats and the mink, and they had a big watermelon. And they cut it up, and started to eat, and I could see it was red as a sunset in June.

J.C. couldn't take his eyes away, a fox loves watermelon so. And after a while the gray fox began throwing us pieces, just to torment us again. We each had a chunk, but Judge Black saw J.C.'s face.

"You take mine, J.C.," he said. "I'm not hungry today." Though I'd watched him that morning swallowing little stones to keep his stomach from shrinking to nothing.

And the watermelon was down J.C.'s throat before you could say swallow.

That night the rabbit was on sentry post, and he woke me and Judge Black just after dawn. He was white as a lily petal. "Come quick," he said. "I kept fine watch. But J.C. is gone."

I rubbed my eyes, and hurried off with the Judge to the gate. It was still locked, but there was a big hole underneath, with tracks going off to the gray fox's home.

Judge Black looked and wiped a tear from his eye. "Better the sting of a scorpion than the daggers of ingratitude," he said.

We didn't mention J.C's name after he left, it made us feel so bad.

A week passed, and then at dawn there was a scratching at the gate. I looked out and saw J.C., with his head bowed like he was praying. "I've come back," he said. "I can't betray my friends."

From then on he was a changed animal.

Day and night he stood guard, never letting anybody relieve him. I don't believe he slept a wink. Whenever a hard or a dangerous task came up, he'd always volunteer. He'd brought some food with him and it gave us strength to keep going. But he always gave most of his share to the others.

I began to get worried. "You can't keep on this way, J.C.," I said. "Your health's too important to us."

But he wouldn't listen. "It's on my mind all the time how I betrayed you," he'd say. "But I'll make up for it, you'll see."

Pretty soon all the food he'd brought was eaten and he began walking up and down again all night.

The gray fox and the others were eating breakfast outside the stockade one morning when J.C. stood up straight as a tree. "I've decided," he said. "I'm going out to fight him and rid the Bend of him forever. It's the only way."

We begged him not to go, and told him the gray fox wouldn't fight fair. But he threw open the gate, and went up to where the fox was sitting.

He slapped the gray fox in the face with his tail, the way foxes do for an insult. "Get your rats and your mink to move aside," he said. "I'm going to fight you a duel."

The rats and the other animals formed a circle, and the two foxes stepped into the middle. In a minute J.C. had the gray fox on the ground and would have been the winner. And then the gray fox gave a whistle, and the rats and mink and some possums rushed in, and pulled him away.

We dashed out to save him. But it was too late. They already had him out of sight.

A couple of nights later we heard a scratching noise outside, and I gave a shout. "It's J.C. come back," I called, and I raced to the gate. But it was only a couple of big wood beetles, chewing the bark on the logs. And then we heard from the bat that some herons down near Baton Rouge had seen the mink taking him across the Big Marshes and off toward the sea.

So now only four of us were left, the rabbit, and the old frog, and Judge Black, and me.

IV

I GUESS the gray fox would have kept after the four of us if it hadn't been for the storm. It was a frightful storm, the tail end of a hurricane up from the Gulf. It flooded the Bend with three feet of water, and a lot of holes were ruined, and a lot of animals were almost drowned. The fox and the rats didn't bother with us now, they had plenty of other things to make 'em worry. And after talking it over we decided it was safe to leave the stockade.

There'd always been storms and floods, but we'd always had some kind of warning. And a crowd of the animals went to see the old muskrat that told us about them before, and asked why he didn't tell us this one was coming. And he sat back in his hole, and scratched his head, and looked very unhappy.

"Don't blame me," he said. "Blame the gray fox and his sewer rats. I'm just as good a prophet as ever. We muskrats know what's coming from the ground, like water from lakes and rivers. But this was a hurricane, that's a sky flood. And that's a job for the birds. I used to work close with the owls and the crows; you know they're the best birds to tell the weather. But now there aren't any birds here, and I won't make any promises. . . . If you call again will you please wipe your feet outside? I've just gotten this place cleaned up and you've tracked this sticky mud all over."

Well, the animals were really angry at the gray fox and I thought it was a good time to start talking again. They listened, but like I said they were hypnotized, and pretty soon they were the same as if the flood had never happened. Only the fox was more careful now, and he didn't start the trouble with the birds the bat had told me he'd planned, and the three sewer rats weren't following us any more.

And then the winter came, and spring, and the gray fox began feeling smart again. And he looked around and said to the rats and the mink, "I've been thinking. We need more room. The Bend here's getting too crowded."

There was a place near us called Cottontail Valley where nobody lived but some rabbits. It was really beautiful, with a big cottonwood grove and long stretches of grass and sweet clover. And he started training the soldiers again, and drove the rabbits out. And there was a fine island in the river called Turkeyfoot, full of live oaks and Spanish moss, with nobody except some wild hogs. Those wild hogs are tough and they fought hard when the fox and the others came. But the rats chewed matches and set fire to the woods, and the hogs swam off down the river. And the gray fox took over Turkeyfoot the way he did Cottontail. And everybody said he was wonderful, like they did before.

And of course he got worse stuck up than ever. He'd found a big mirror they'd thrown out at the farm with a wide crack in the middle. And he'd sit before it and look at himself and fluff out his tail by the hour. And then he'd turn to a rat or a mink and say, "When I was down at the Zoo in New Orleans," or "That reminds me of the time I fought the forty two dogs when I lost my eye."

It was quiet now for a little while, with some lovely sunny days, but it didn't brighten our spirits.

And then the young raccoons I'd invited

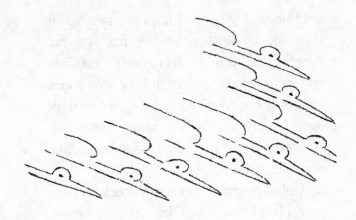

last year came to see me again, but I had to
send them away.

"I can't be responsible for you," I told
them. "Something may happen here any
minute."

Judge Black nodded sadly. "I was in the
woods yesterday," he said. "And I saw the
bees moving out of the old cottonwood tree
where they'd lived for a hundred years. And
I asked 'em why and they said there were

such terrible things coming to the Bend they didn't want to be around here any more."

We watched the young raccoons go down the bank. And it made us feel much worse.

And then the gray fox remembered the birds. He and the rats began crossing the sand ridge onto the half of the Bend where the birds had gone, and stole all the fruit and every egg they could find. And the birds were furious because the fox had broken his word. They liked to wait till a mink came over, and then they'd swoop and make big

scratches in his fur. And the mink would go almost crazy, because his fur was so valuable.

And the fox would puff himself up and his face would get red as a strawberry. "It's becoming very clear," he said one day. "I'll have to finish what I started last year. There's not room for both of us and the birds in the Bend."

He began training the animals every minute. Often he kept 'em drilling and marching all night. And he even got some red ants to come and show 'em how to march, because ants are the best soldiers of all. And then one day a whole army of wharf and sewer rats came up from New Orleans, I guess maybe a couple of hundred. The fox said they were running from the exterminators, but I knew it wasn't so.

That night the little bat flew over and woke me. He hung straight up on a branch and I could see he was all upset. He started to talk and then he made an awful face, like he was almost dying. "This horrible thing's coming over me again," he said. "I don't know whether I'm bird or animal. And it's the same with all the bats. I may break off talking in the middle."

He swung upside down to rest himself, and then swung back again. "I was just flying around the gray fox's camp and I heard him talking to the rats. He's almost ready to declare war on the birds to drive 'em out of all the swamp. And the same way as it was before, he won't have anybody that's against him around. He's coming to get you and the others tomorrow. He's —"

All of a sudden he made a terrible face again, and turned and flew off into the woods. But he'd told us all we needed to know, and I waked the others in a hurry, and rushed them into the stockade. We patched up a few breaks in the wood and cleared out the weeds, and then we slammed the gate. We watched all day, but not a rat or a mink came near us.

"I'll bet you the bat was wrong," said the rabbit. "It's hotter here than last year. Let's open the gate and go out."

But Judge Black and I talked to him, and persuaded him to stay inside.

Well, the sun went down, and still nothing happened. And then some frogs that the gray fox had brought started singing outside, practicing "Old Oaken Bucket." But it was the most terrible frog singing you ever heard, with not a single note in tune.

Our old frog covered up his ears, and then he hopped toward the gate. "It's driving me crazy," he croaked. "They sing *fa* when it ought to be *do*, and they sing *re* and *mi* together. I've got to show 'em how to do it right or my ears'll crack."

I tried to stop him because I knew it was a trick. The frog was slow most of the time, but when it came to music he was lightning.

And before I could get there he'd squeezed under the gate, and in a second the rats and mink rushed out, and the old frog was missing.

And then next morning they began with the rabbit. And of course he didn't have much sense. They dug a nice rabbit hole and I saw them put something inside.

The rabbit gave a long sniff, and his tail began to wag like a cotton boll in the wind. He hadn't had a good meal for months. "There's carrots," he giggled. "And lettuce. And I think I smell celery, too. You could take the lettuce first, and after that eat the carrots. And then you could have the celery stalks. It'd make a wonderful three course dinner."

And when another daybreak came the rabbit wasn't with us anymore.

So that left just Judge Black and me.

They tried to catch the Judge a dozen times. And once I thought they'd succeeded.

One afternoon we saw a baby chipmunk in front of the stockade, tied to a bush with a piece of vine, and squealing terribly. The fox 'd put the chipmunk there because he knew the Judge couldn't see anything suffer. The Judge watched awhile, and then couldn't stand it any longer. He ran out and began to untie the vine, and then the rats and the mink came racing. But he snatched the baby in his mouth, and in a flash was back in the stockade. Of course they tried to catch me, too. But I was too smart for 'em, so after a while they got tired of trying.

We'd found an old rabbit hole that led from the stockade to a hollow tree, right by where the fox held his meetings. And we dug it out so we could get food or hide in the trunk and see what was happening. We'd been in it only a few times when they learned about it some way. We had crawled to the end and Judge Black was just coming outside when I saw the rats and the mink jump on him—they must have been waiting for hours. And then I saw him wriggle away and race toward the woods, with half a dozen mink right after. And I was sick with worry because it looked to me like he was hurt in the back. And that'd be very dangerous, because he'd been hurt there before. A snake's back is so long and delicate, and he hurts there so easy.

I rushed out so the mink 'd follow me and let him get away. And I ran through a canebrake till I threw 'em off the track, and then I started looking. I looked through the woods and the pasture behind the farm, searching under logs and down holes. But I couldn't find him anywhere, and I got more and more afraid.

I saw a lady alligator beside a pool, squirting water on the earth where her eggs were buried so the sun 'd make steam for 'em to hatch, and I asked her if she had seen anything.

She shook her head. "I'm a good mother but not very bright," she said. "They tell me we alligators haven't a brain. Just an air pocket in our head. I can't remember anything, even for a few minutes. I think I remember a blacksnake going toward the cornfield at the end of the farm a while ago, but I can't be sure. And I think I remember the way he crawled that he was badly hurt."

I went to the cornfield but I couldn't dis-

cover a thing. I went into a hundred holes, I guess, some that hadn't been used for years. And then I saw one with marks around it where a snake had just gone down, and I hurried in to find out. And then I heard a fearful rattling, and I saw a dozen big rattle-snakes lined against the walls. And in front of them a rattler was coiled, with his tail shaking like crazy.

"I'm looking for Judge Black, the black-snake," I said. "Have any of you seen him around?"

A big diamond-back near me made his forked tongue quiver, and he hissed, and the other snakes hissed, too. "You're the fifth animal that's asked that question to-day," he said. "There've been two rats and a mink and a possum before you. I'll thank you not to bother us anymore. We've got a visitor here, on his way West from the Kentucky hills. He's giving us an exhibition of the dance he's going to perform at the Snake

Dance out in Arizona. . . . If you want to find your snake, go to Dismal Swamp down the river. That's where snakes around here always go when there's trouble."

It was late in the afternoon now, and I went toward Dismal Swamp, like he'd said. It was an awful swamp, where regular animals wouldn't go, only alligators and moccasins and big whipsnakes that beat you to death. It was night when I got there and thousands of mosquitos were flying around, so thick it was like a fog. And I scratched a turpentine tree the way bears do, and took the gum, and spread it over my fur. And the mosquitoes didn't bother me anymore. They hated turpentine gum because if they touched me they'd stick, just like I was a flypaper.

And then I began to search in the dark, down the cottonmouth and rattler holes and the tangles of poison oak and palmetto. And sometimes I'd have to rest, and I'd look up

at the stars. And I was lonelier than I'd ever been in my life. I'd seen my friends disappear, one by one. And now Judge Black was gone, and he was my best friend of all. And I'd think how he was lying hurt under the trees, and maybe the mink had killed him. And I'd stand up, and put more turpentine gum on my face, and start searching again.

Morning came, and I was afraid I'd have to give up, when I saw a wild duck with his green feathers all ragged and broken. His eyes were sad, but he had a good face, and he was the first nice thing I'd seen for hours. He came up and asked if he could help.

"They call me The Hermit of Dismal Swamp," he said. "Maybe you've heard about me. Years ago I was a decoy duck for the hunters. I'd sit in a pond till some ducks came to join me, and then the hunters would find 'em. And one day the other ducks caught me and put me here in the swamp, and said if I ever flew out they'd kill me. I'm here in prison for life. I don't blame the ducks for what they did. But I wasn't too much to blame either. I was young and when you're young you make mistakes. Only my mistake was terrible. . . . You're the first animal or bird I've spoken to for over a year."

I talked to him for a while and told him why I'd come.

His sad eyes brightened a little. "I saw the blacksnake late yesterday," he said. "I'm sure it's the one you're hunting. He was in those big cypress trees, over along the bayou. He looked as if he was badly hurt. He can't have gone far away."

He led me through the cypress woods, and then I saw the Judge, caught in a piece of barbed wire fence that'd been washed down the bayou. And he was lying so still for a minute I thought he wasn't breathing. But I twisted him free, and pulled him up on the bank, and he opened his eyes and smiled. "I knew you'd find me," he said. "It's a long lane that has no turning."

I saw a snake doctor flying around, and I called him and he came over. And he worked for a while and said the Judge 'd be all right. One of the mink had bitten him in the back, like I thought, but it hadn't gone deep in the bone. And the decoy duck fixed up a bed of grass and leaves, and brought him the roots to chew the snake doctor ordered, and in a few days he was fine.

We started to go back to the river, and I thanked the duck for what he had done.

His feathers were smoother now and he looked happier. "I'm glad if by helping the Judge I've helped the birds," he said. "I hope I can help them again. If you see any wild ducks tell them you met me. And tell them that day and night I sit among the alligators, being sorry for the wrong that I've done."

The Judge told him to think of something more cheerful. "A bad beginning can sometimes make a good ending," he said.

We made our way to the Bend. And we thought we'd better not go back to the stockade, now that the fox knew about the hole underneath, so we picked a hole in a tree not far away where we could watch what he was doing.

There'd been the biggest fight of all with the birds while we were away. And we hadn't been back more than a few hours when there was a great flapping of wings in the sky, and a big flock of birds circled over. And then the eagle and the owl flew down where the fox and the rats were waiting. And all the other birds, the herons and the geese, and the bluejays and the crows, all took their places behind 'em.

The eagle's eyes were stern and his voice was cold. "I've come for the last time," he said. "We birds are very peaceful. We gave you half this swamp. But you've taken our fruit just the same. And you've stolen our eggs and frightened our young. Many of them will be marked for life. It can't keep on this way."

The old owl was shaking worse than ever and now his whole head jerked with his eye. "I'm so nervous a caterpillar can make me jump out of my feathers," he said. "We can't even teach our young owls to fly, and this is the training season. Accidents every day, and only last night two young barn owls broke their wings."

The eagle's eyes flashed fire. "We're very patient, we birds. But if you and your animals don't change your ways, I warn you, we'll deal with you harshly."

The birds all set up a terrific cawing and honking they agreed, and the woodpeckers hammered on the trees. And the poor owl looked so pitiful they might have been hammering on his skull.

The fox sat quiet for a minute, and then he smiled his oily smile. "I'm sorry my animals got out of control," he said. "But it's warm weather and high spirits. You know how it is. I'll see it doesn't happen any more. . . . Have some of these mangoes if you care for fruit. Some friends just brought 'em off a ship that came in at New Orleans."

The eagle looked pleased and ate a piece, and then he and the other birds flew off. And when they were out of sight the fox's face changed, like day changes to night.

"I wasn't going to start the war for a couple of weeks," he said. "But now we won't wait. We'll attack at sunrise tomorrow."

Well, there was a lot of sharpening of teeth, and practicing how they'd act in the fighting. And just before daybreak they

started out with the fox at the head, waving his tail. And we went behind where they couldn't see us, dodging through the trees and the bushes.

Just as the sun came up they crossed the sand ridge, into the other half of the Bend. The rats and the others stayed hidden in the woods, and the fox went up to the tall pine where the eagle had his nest, and knocked at the bottom of the trunk.

The eagle put out his head, so high you could hardly see. "Who's there?" he called.

"It's me," said the

fox, and his voice was like molasses. "We've got a carrier pigeon fell down on our side of the swamp late yesterday. He said he was carrying a message for you from Washington. We thought it was important." He held up a pigeon he'd brought.

"That's really nice of you," called the eagle. "I guess they want me to do some more posing."

He flew down in front of the fox. "I want to apologize for the way I spoke yesterday," he said. "I thought—"

He never finished the sentence. He'd walked right into a trap. They'd made a net of vines like hunters use and hidden it in the grass. The eagle struggled to get loose, but it only pulled the net closer. And in a minute the fox and the others had him tied till he couldn't move even a feather.

The fox's tail swelled to twice its size with pride. "We've caught the king of the birds," he said. "The war's as good as won."

And then some possums came out carrying a cage they'd made of chicken wire
stolen from the farm. And they put the eagle
inside, and started marching through the
woods. And the other animals marched behind, just like it was a funeral. And the birds
came to find out what was happening. And
then they saw the eagle tied, with big tears
dropping from his eyes, and they stood like
they were birds made of iron. And then the
rats and the mink and the possums began to
drive them back. With the eagle in the cage
most of the birds hadn't the heart to fight at
all. Only once in a while a flock of crows or

hawks or blackbirds maybe would fly up and come charging forward. And then the animals would come yelping and howling and the birds would be forced back farther and farther.

Twilight came and a lot of bats flew out, and at first I thought they were going to help the birds, and then I saw they were helping the rats and the possums. And that was an awful thing because there was so many. When the crows and the rest would start to attack, the bats would block the way with their big wings, and the birds couldn't do anything. By midnight the birds were all driven out of the Bend, across a narrow bayou. It was a dreadful place where there'd been a big forest fire, with nothing but burned trees and ashes.

The gray fox stopped at the edge of the water, and looked across, and his face was proud. "The war's over. We've won the Bend," he said.

And the rats and the mink gave a cheer, and put out guards, and went to sleep for the night.

I stayed with Judge Black in the bushes a long time, thinking. And then I knew what I'd do. And I left the  Judge to keep watch, and crossed to the burned woods where the birds were staying. It was spooky there with all those black trunks and branches. And every step you took would raise a puff of ashes. Once in a while you'd see a bird sitting like a ghost. And then a burned tree would fall, and it'd sound like ghost thunder.

I found the old owl on a blackened log, and I told him everything wasn't lost. I told him that he was next to the eagle and that he ought to pull the birds together. But he was too worn out now to even shake, and he looked gloomy as a buzzard.

"I don't want to take command," he answered. "I only took this job to help out. Just as an assistant. I know I have the reputation of being wise. But I can't think of anything. Besides I can tell when I'm beaten. I'm going away with any birds that want to come, maybe to the Bad Lands of South Dakota."

I talked and argued and told him I'd help, and finally he said he'd try. And then I went off and found the little bat hanging in his tree, and he was crying worse than before.

"We shouldn't have helped the animals," he sobbed. "But we had a vote and the animals won. It was a terrible thing to do."

I asked him to take me to the cave where the bats lived. And after a few minutes he looked better, and started flying before me. "They'll never talk to you hanging straight up," he said. "If it bothers you too much there's no other way for you except to stand on your head."

We came to the cave way back of the swamp, and there were hundreds of bats, maybe thousands. And they were all upside down and it made me very dizzy. There was a big lady bat that seemed to be the boss. And she was holding a baby upside down, too, and it made me dizzier than ever. But I didn't look at her for a minute and that made things easier. I told her and the others that even if the bats were part animal, any animal part like the fox was bad. It was better now to think about their wings, and just remember they were birds.

"I agree," she said. "This is the worst thing in my lifetime. But with bats majority rules, and there's an old bat here that's very stubborn. We voted once but we'll vote again. I'll do whatever I can."

I left and I heard 'em arguing in their squeaky little voices. And then I went off to

Sugar Cane, the little town below the swamp where I had something very important to see about, and I didn't get back till near sunrise.

And then I joined Judge Black again and we sneaked over where the fox and the rats were camped, and sat and waited. And as soon as it started growing light, I saw a cloud of birds rising over the burned trees, and I knew the old owl hadn't failed us. The fox saw the cloud, too, and knew what it meant, and then the battle began. First the wood-peckers came and they'd jump on a rat or a mink or a possum and tap till he was running in circles. And after that the blackbirds and crows 'd dive down like airplanes and scratch and pull out hair, and the hawks and owls 'd follow, pecking and screaming. A minute later the water birds came, the her-ons and cranes and a few pelicans up from the marshes. They spread out in a wide line and went marching forward, with their big

beaks clashing like knives. A lot of the animals broke and ran when they saw those
fearful beaks coming, and the birds began
driving 'em toward the main part of the
Bend. But the rats whipped the animals back,
and they stood steady again. And then I saw
the bats wheel out of the woods like smoke
and start helping the gray fox, with a big bat
wrinkled as an old cypress tree leading 'em
on. And then I saw the lady bat and the little

bat I knew rush up to the old bat, and they
started an awful argument. And the old bat
finally gave a furious squeak and flew away.
And then all the bats swung around and
started fighting for
the birds.

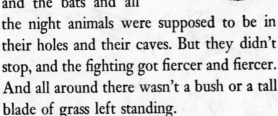

It was a terrible bat-
tle, and the two armies
would sweep back and
forth, just like the
waves of the sea. The
sun was high in the
sky now, and the owls
and the bats and all
the night animals were supposed to be in
their holes and their caves. But they didn't
stop, and the fighting got fiercer and fiercer.
And all around there wasn't a bush or a tall
blade of grass left standing.

And suddenly I heard the fox give a command, and an army of rats came marching
down in a solid line, keeping step like they

were made of clocksprings and wood. They stopped opposite a big grove of pines on the other bank where the trees hadn't been burned. And then they got ready to swim across, and I could see they were all chewing matches.

The old owl gave a dreadful cry. "They've found out where we've hidden our eggs and our young ones that can't fly!" he shouted. "They're going to set fire to the woods! There won't be any young birds any more!"

The birds started to panic now, and broke ranks to get to their children. And then another army of rats came down the bank right after the first, and they were chewing matches, too. And then I turned and looked behind me, and gave a signal. And the rats looked, too, and started running so fast it was their tails, not the matches that almost caught fire. There were a hundred cats, the biggest tomcats I could find in Sugar Cane, gray toms and black toms, and brindles and yellows, toms from the feed stores and the butcher shops, toms from the fish cannery and the dairy barns, all with big scars on their faces and chewed up tails, the toughest cats on the river. All I had to do was to tell 'em about the rats at the Bend, and of course they stopped whatever work they were doing and came with me to the swamp.

Well, you can imagine what happened. The rats jumped into holes and climbed up trees, and crawled under roots and stones.

And then the birds saw their children were safe, and came back to the battle. And then we found the cage with the eagle in some bushes, and we cut him free. And in a few minutes the mink and the possums and all the rest were running faster than the rats.

And then I saw the fox and the rat that was his friend racing toward their camp. And the hawks and the owls swept down and drove them into the tangles of thorn bushes and palmetto. The thorns were bad enough but the pheasants and the big wild turkeys in the brush flew at them wherever they turned, and they ran into the open again. The hawks drove 'em to the river now, and a lot more of the big land birds were lined up on the bank, and hundreds of the little birds like the robins and wrens they'd always tormented so. And each bird took a peck as they passed.

The fox and the rat tried to escape by jumping in the river and swimming. But the

big water birds were waiting, and drove 'em back to the birds on the shore. And then a woodpecker hopped onto the rat, and two of 'em hopped onto the head of the fox, and they began hammering and laughing like they were crazy. And then the eagle jumped onto the fox's back and began nipping his ears and twisting his tail, and the eagle began laughing, too. And all the birds laughed so hard, you couldn't have heard it thunder.

The fox and the rat ran hollering down

the bank, with the woodpeckers hammering faster and faster. And then they swung around a bend. And that was the last of 'em we saw.

I was worried after all the rats were gone when I saw the cats smiling and being terribly polite to the birds. So I thanked 'em fast, and they thanked me, and then they all went home.

In the afternoon we found a couple of mink hiding in a hole, and we made 'em tell us what had happened to J.C. and the others. They hadn't been killed as we were afraid. The gray fox had put 'em off in a cave a little way down the river. We found 'em, and they were terribly thin. But we fed 'em all the fine things to eat the gray fox had hidden away, cheese and sausages and fruit the rats stole in the fancy stores at New Orleans. And in a little while they were as good as before.

Then one by one the animals that'd left

us for the gray fox started coming back and apologizing. And they asked us if we'd let things be like they were before, and of course we said yes. We knew it'd been just a kind of sickness.

And then about a week later the birds gave me what they call a testimonial dinner. And all the birds and animals were there, and the eagle and the owl and Judge Black made long speeches, and the crow had come back and he made a speech, too, and we all had a wonderful time. There was a little trouble for a few minutes in the middle when the little bat started crying again, saying that maybe he'd done the wrong thing after all. But we got him cheered up all right. And then the crow's sister got all excited because she thought she'd laid an egg in a truck loaded with hay that was going to Memphis. But then she remembered she'd put it in a squirrel hole right next to her nest. And everything was better than ever.

I wondered for a long while what'd happened to the gray fox. And then one day I heard a rumor. And not long after I hopped into a big farmer's truck loaded with vegetables he was taking to New Orleans. While he was in the market, I went off to the Zoo. And there sure enough, like I'd heard, was the gray fox in a cage, talking and fluffing out his tail, while all the other animals sat and listened, just like he was a king. "Now when I was at Catfish Bend," he was saying.

ᶒᶒᶒᶒᶒᶒᶒᶒᶒᶒᶒᶒᶒᶒᶒᶒᶒᶒᶒᶒᶒᶒ

The raccoon finished his story and took a couple of the licorice drops I pulled out of my pocket.

A dozen or so foxes were rushing around near the river with J.C. in charge, carrying stones and digging a wide, shallow hole. And a few herons and cranes were standing alongside, every now and then giving advice. It was terribly hot in the sun, and often a fox would come to the river bank and splash some water over his face, and then hurry back.

I asked why they were working so hard on such a hot day.

The raccoon put one of the candies in his mouth and hid the other under a log. "Every anniversary they build something nice for the birds to make 'em forget," he said. "This year they're giving the land birds a bird bath and the water birds a fine wading pool."

Some other Puffin books are
described on the following pages.

Ben Lucien Burman

HIGH WATER AT CATFISH BEND

This is the hilarious story of how animals in a Mississippi flood take over the problem of flood control from incompetent human beings. Doc Raccoon, strategist and statesman; Judge Black, the kindly, motto-quoting black snake; J.C., the clever fox; and all the rest of the population of Catfish Bend go from one surprise to another while the water rises. As readers young and old will learn, the story's appeal is universal, for here are animal saints and animal villains, animal generals and animal clowns, animal sages and animal snobs —all in a rollicking parody of humanity. With delightful illustrations by Alice Caddy.

Michael Bond

THE TALES OF OLGA DA POLGA

Some of these adventures of a lovable guinea pig who has truly amazing talents really happened; others are figments of Olga's (and of Michael Bond's) imagination. In any case Olga will endear herself to parents and children alike. Illustrated by Hans Helwig.

OLGA MEETS HER MATCH

Here are more of Olga's astonishing adventures. First there is Noel's disappearance, then the strange business of the dragon, and finally the terrifying threat to Olga's new friend, Venables the toad.... Once again, Hans Helwig's delightful illustrations add to the fun.

E. Nesbit

THE STORY OF THE TREASURE SEEKERS

The six Bastable children try everything they can think of to restore their family's fortune . . . from digging for treasure to being detectives. This lighthearted adventure story has a surprise ending. Illustrated by Cecil Leslie.

THE WOULDBEGOODS

After a particularly bad escapade, the Bastables are sent away to the country . . . to a house with a real water-filled moat around it. They form a society called "The Wouldbegoods," because they would be good if only they could, but the moat offers exciting new adventures. Illustrated by Cecil Leslie.

FIVE CHILDREN AND IT

Five children find a thousand-year-old Psammead in a sandpit. "It" grants them one wish each day, but what-ever they wish for must vanish at sunset. Illustrated by H. R. Millar.

THE PHOENIX AND THE CARPET

Here are more adventures of the five children. This time, a carpet bought for their nursery turns out to have magic powers. Illustrated by H. R. Millar.

THE STORY OF THE AMULET

The five children travel back through time to ancient Egypt and Babylon in search of the missing half of a magic amulet. Illustrated by H. R. Millar.

Norman Hunter

THE PECULIAR TRIUMPH OF PROFESSOR BRANESTAWM

Here are more adventures of eccentric old Professor Branestawm, who now invents a translating machine, a getting-you-dressed machine, and a Stratospheric Limousine. This new book of stories finds the professor in as many hilarious predicaments as the two earlier volumes, *The Incredible Adventures of Professor Branestawm* and *Professor Branestawm's Treasure Hunt*. George Adamson's delightful illustrations add to the fun. Norman Hunter is also the author of *The Puffin Book of Magic*.